I0765547

NO FEAR

by

Lynda Rees

COPYRIGHT©

DEDICATION

This book is dedicated to my grandchildren,
Harley Sage Nelson,
Hunter Michael Nelson and
Easton James Rees.
Walk through life fearlessly.
Lead long, healthy and
Productive lives
Brimming with fun,
Laughter and overflowing
With love.
You have all of mine.

MamMa

Bear cub, Gus crawled from the cave Mommy Bear had left him sleeping in. "I'm hungry and lonely."

He wandered through the forest. Soon he was lost and scared. He'd never been so far before.

He sniffed back tears. Something smelled good.

"Mommy's going to be mad when she sees I got lost."

His belly rumbled. "Yum, those red balls smell sweet enough to eat." He raced toward the bush.

Branches overhead rustled. Birds chirped and flew away. A barking, hissing, shrieking growl startled Gus. A screeching, guttural noise sent him skidding in his rush to get to the yummy fruit.

Jumping back, he stumbled over a log and fell onto his butt. His feet smashed into the bush. Berries fell atop his belly.

Laughter sounded from behind a nearby tree. A deer fawn stuck his head out. Beneath the fawn, a young raccoon, a baby rabbit and a tiny skunk peered out.

Gus propped on elbows. "Hey, what are you laughing at?"

The deer snickered. "Sorry, we couldn't help it."

"You look hilarious." The skunk twitched her nose.

The others jumped and hid, as Gus growled. "You might as well come out. I know you're there."

Quivering, the fawn stepped into the clearing, looking ready to flee. "Sorry about that."

Gus's head tilted. He trembled, and his fur shook.

The buck fawn laughed. "Are you scared?"

"Who me? I'm not afraid of anything." Gus sat up.

"Yeah you are." The raccoon bared his teeth fiercely.

Gus jumped back a bit.

"You look scared." The rabbit flapped his long ears.

"Yep, definitely afraid." The skunk spun and aimed her fluffy tail at Gus but didn't spray.

"So what? You look frightened too." Gus showed his fangs.

"I am . . . a little, but Mommy said I'll grow up to be King of The Woods." The fawn held his head high.

"Huh, that's a joke. I'll be a huge bear someday. I'll be King of The Woods." Gus flexed his claws.

"Moms have big dreams." The rabbit's nose twitched.

The deer pawed the ground, snorting. "Mommy said I'll jump high fences and run fast. My head will grow a huge rack, to show I'm king."

Gus admired Dash's speckled back. "I'll be bigger than my mommy when I grow up."

"Can we get this contest over?" The skunk rolled her eyes.

The raccoon stood on hind legs. "My name's Dex. We could be friends . . . if you won't hurt us."

Gus laughed. "I'd like that. Why would I hurt you? I'd be alone."

Dash snorted. "Bears eat smaller creatures. They like meat."

Gus scowled. "Yuck! I 'd never eat an animal friend."

The rabbit's nose wiggled. "I'm Hal. The skunk is Sadie."

"My name's Gus. It's nice to meet you." Gus wasn't lonely any longer. His insides felt happy.

Dex walked to the river and washed his food.

Gus stared. "Why does he do that?"

"It's a compulsive habit with Dex's kind." Sadie smiled.

"We call it cleanliness." Adorable Dex stood on hind legs.

"It looks like Dex is begging." Gus chuckled.

"Or waving," Hal added.

"Sadie, that white strip looks like it was painted down your pretty tail." Dash snorted happily.

"Thank you. It's a warning sign. When I'm about three months old, I'll be able to spray a nasty scent at anything that scares me." Sadie's chest puffed out proudly.

"That stink takes forever to wear off." Hal steered clear of her rear.

"Don't spray me." Gus sniffed her tail. "You have a musky odor back there."

Sadie acted sassy. "We all have defensive skills."

"What about Hal?" Gus studied his buddy.

"Close your eyes." Hal snickered. Gus put paws over them, and Hal slipped into the bushes. "Look."

Gus opened his eyes. "Wow, if I wasn't searching I'd never see you."

Hal laughed. "I have keen senses and see far distances clearly. I freeze in place, and others don't notice me."

"That's cool. Dex, I heard how you protect yourself. Your screeching would scare anyone." Gus pointed to Dex, who stood on hind legs, rocking shoulders.

Dash grinned. "I'll have strong legs and sharp hooves to help me jump high and run like the wind. Mommy said they're also for combat. It's good to be able to fight when you must, but better to avoid battle and get far away from danger."

Distant rustling sounded. Thudding shook the ground and grew closer. Birds squawked and flew away, rustling tree leaves. The young animals jerked to attention.

Hal whispered, "Danger's coming."

Gus's nose went up with a sniff. "Mommy's looking for me."

Dex glared at Gus. "Your mom won't settle for fruit when there's meat."

Sadie's voice grew shrill. "We've got to run."

Dash's tail twitched. "I'm out of here." He jumped and ran.

"Me too." Hal slipped into the brush. Dex scampered away.

"I won't let her eat you. See you soon." Gus waved sadly as his friends disappeared.

Mommy Bear thumped into the clearing. "There you are, Little One. I was worried about you."

Gus handed her a paw full of berries. "I got hungry. Want some?"

"Thank you." She lapped the berries with her big tongue. "Delicious."

"Mommy, do bears eat meat?" Gus cocked his head.

"Yes, Gus, we need protein to keep us fat and sassy."

"I like berries." Eating meat didn't sound good to Gus.

"Fruit doesn't have protein and fat we require to stay healthy."

"Isn't there something we can eat other than creatures?" Gus plopped onto his bottom.

"There's fish." Mommy put an arm around Gus.

"Great, I'll eat fruit and fish—not meat." It was a better idea. Gus didn't know any fish.

Mommy Bear lifted her cub's chin with her great paw. "You're a peculiar little guy, Gus. I love you. I need to teach you to be a skilled fisher."

"That would be super, Mommy." Gus romped joyfully. "I'll make you proud, Mommy. I'll be the best fishing bear in the forest."

Mommy Bear turned and started walking. "Come; I heard bees swarming over the hill. I'll teach you to steal honey."

"Do I have to kill bees?" Gus followed.
He'd never eaten honey.

"No, Gus; and you'll love honey."

"I love all sorts of things about the forest. I learned a lot today."

"Good, what did you learn?" Mommy grinned.

"Scary things aren't frightening when you get to know them; and everyone is different in some special way."

"That's my boy." Mommy smiled proudly.

It was a good day in the forest.

THE END

If you have pre-teen readers, you'll want them to read *Freckle Face & Blondie and The Thinking Tree*, two lovely mystery novels that teach youngsters to love reading, think about the world around them and develop reasoning skills.

Freckle Face & The Thinking Tree
By Harley Nelson and Lynda Rees

Preteens, Freckle Face and Blondie solve a missing person's case and start a private investigation business as small-town heroines.

AND

The Thinking Tree
By Harley Nelson and Lynda Rees

Preteen, private investigators solve a disappearing jewel case and locate a missing loved one.

Get them at: www.lyndareesauthor.com

ALSO BY LYNDA REES:

Middle-Grade Children:
  Freckle Face & Blondie
  The Thinking Tree
Children's Picture Book: NO FEAR
Historical Romance: Gold Lust Conspiracy

Mystery:
  God Father's Day
  Madam Mom
  2nd Chance Ranch
  Hart's Girls
  Operation Second Chance
  The Bloodline Series:
                  Leah's Story
          Parsley, Sage, Rose, Mary & Wine
                  Blood & Studs
                  Hot Blooded
                  Blood of Champions
                  Bloodlines & Lies
                  Horseshoes & Roses
                  The Bloodline Trail
                  Real Money
                  The Bourbon Trail

Find Lynda's books at: www.lyndareesauthor.com

ABOUT LYNDA REES:

Lynda is a multi-award-winning author from Kentucky. Her works span from historical conspiracy theory novels, to contemporary romance, cozy romantic mysteries, suspense, children's middle-grade, children's picture books and non-fiction. Lynda is published in novels, business, advertising and freelance.

She'd love a review from you. Reviews are extremely important to Lynda, as an author. Please leave a book review.

Lynda can be reached at her website, via email or you can become a **VIP** to get **FREE** reads, exclusive offers and gifts.

The End